Stories Of

HAPPILY

EVER

AFTER

WRITTEN BY

JOHN SUMMER

First published in 2022 by
BecomeShakespeare.com

One Point Six Technologies Pvt Ltd.
119-123, 1st Floor, Building J2, B - Wing, WadalaTruck Terminal,
Wadala East, Mumbai, Maharashtra, India, 400022.
T:+91 8080226699

ISBN: 978-93-5610-269-9

DEDICATED TO ALL MY READERS

What is a fairytale ? For the answer lies everywhere.

- John Summer

Contents

1

PRINCESS SCARLET, THE WITCH, AND THE FIRE MOUNTAIN

The celebration for nuptials between Prince Fredrick and Princess Scarlet was no ordinary-abundant with feast, drinks, music, and ball. Every King and Queen from all the Kingdoms were invited. The Princesses adored and complimented each other's dress and hair and flirted with the princes of other Kingdoms. Children were in their jovial world playing with the dancing fountains on the lawn. It was morning in mid-summer, Our King Lucifus was leaping between guests in a joyous mood but our adventurous Princess Scarlet was far away, riding through the cornfields that stretched all the way to the pine forest. She rode beside river rhine down the shadowy mountains before arriving at a hamlet nearby. Scarlet entered the hamlet incognito and took shelter with the village chief's family. The chief questioned her, where are you going?

'I'm on my way to visit my niece who lives in the town on the other side of the mountain'. Was Scarlet's reply.

But the chief knew there was no town nearby just mountains all the way. He advises her not to venture to the east.

'The forest down there-it's creepy and deceiving. Many things happened there'. He said.

Scarlet didn't know what that meant. She stayed in the hamlet for two days. Realizing someone from the Kingdom would come for her and take her away to marry a stodgy Prince, she decides to leave. She wants no one but Prince charming to come and take her away. Her mother used to tell her it happens only in fairytales. The next day our insouciant Princess rides to the east. Meanwhile, in the castle, there is an uproar about the Princess being kidnapped. Prince Fredrick took it upon himself to bring back the Princess.

'I give my word, my King . I'll bring back my betrothe'. Saying he rode taking with him his few trusted men.

A few miles down east, surrounded by lush green forest Scarlet meets a shepherd boy of her age. As it was already getting dark, Scarlet takes shelter in his shack. Both relinquished their appetite with some bread and hot tea. He too advises her not to go further into the forest.

'A fire-skinned monster crawl in one of the mountains'. He warned her.

She slept and woke up early to find that the boy was gone. She waited till the sun was at zenith. Making up her mind she rode again further into the forest, also called the whistling woods. Prince Fredrick passed the village chief's hamlet, who said Scarlet left from here three days ago. With his men, he continued to ride east following tracks leading to the whistling woods. Dark and cold Scarlet made her way through cramped and twisted trees when a dark-robed woman carrying a lamp stopped her. The woman lures Scarlet deep into the woods where she chains her up inside the fire mountain. The woman reveals that she once loved Scarlet's father but he abandoned her after finding out that she was a witch. Betrayed she tried to seek revenge twice. First when King Lucifus got married and the second time when Scarlet was born.

But now luck was in favour of the witch. The witch explained as Scarlet senses something crawling up, that's when she saw huge eyes glowing with fire staring at her. She screamed.

A mile away Prince Fredrick sees the fire mountain and rides quickly. Inside a loud shriek echoed as the monster was defeated and so was the witch. Prince Fredrick rescued Princess Scarlet just when the fire mountain came crumbling down with blaze. His fellow men held their swords high savouring victory. Out from the rubble emerged the shepherd boy. He said it was the witch who turned him into a monster. Finally freed the shepherd boy leaves thanking Prince Fredrick. Scarlet asked the Prince his name.

'I'm Prince Fredrick of Wurshire'. He said.

'I can call you, Freddy. Scarlet said beaming. Back in the castle, they get married like in a fairytale and live happily forever.

2

THE INVISIBLE TOWER OF MALKITH

The celebration was reaching sky-high in Kingdom Nimbad. King Edwardel was brushed his feet off visiting guests and elites who came from far away Kingdom for his daughter's wedding. The King entered his daughter's room.

'Father, how do I look'. Exclaimed Helena.

'Ahhh. you're not ready yet. Everybody is waiting down'. The King said rushing himself.

'Father, the dress'. Helena repeated.

'Oh! yes'. Calming himself he sighed. 'I didn't know my daughter looked so beautiful. Now be prompt, the Prince is due to come anytime now'. Again rushing he left.

A guard stopped the King on his way. 'sire, Izus is here'.

The King's face turned red. Izus was a wizard none liked, he just performed tricks on occasion to entertain the folks of the

Kingdom. King Edwardel knew Izus is here just not for some tricks. He stormed into the long-empty hall and saw Izus waiting there facing the other side.

'Now what do you want, Izus. I don't want any tricks on my daughter's wedding'. Kings cowled. The wizard turned with a stern look.

'That's not what wizard always do, sire'. He said in a mocking tone. 'I need what I always wanted and you'll get me that'.

'I've told you many times before what you seek-'.

Before he could finish Izus waved his hand as some guards marched in. They took the King away and locked him up in a dungeon. Princess Helena heard some hurly-burly around, startled to see some guards searching for her she hid and secretly slipped to the dungeon to see her father locked inside.

'Father, what is happening'. Helena said panting.

King Edwardel said the Prince won't come because Izus has obstructed their path. He said about the wizard's powers locked somewhere, so he can rule the Kingdom. He told her to escape in a secret tunnel.

'Go to Captain Edmont, cadge him to find the lost tower of Malkith'. That's all he said.

Helena didn't know what that all meant but she obeyed her father and left the castle secretly. Wearing her new golden yellow dress, Helena padded the busy streets of the town. It was dark and nobody recognised her as everyone wore their best dresses for her wedding. She walked down the damp place looking at *people drawing carriages, women wrangling with vendors and two children teasing the dogs. She entered an alley, sat in an empty recess and cried. A beggar passed in front of her.*

'Take this. It's cold'. He said offering his blanket before settling next to his usual recess. 'somethin' goin' at the castle. You comin' from ther ain't you'. He asked.

'I don't know '. She said and slept cuddled.

Helena woke up at the sound of bustling and braying, it was daybreak.

The beggar said. 'the ship has arriv'd, they'r takin' all guds to sell at the ports'.

'How do I get there'. Helena asked frantically.

'Just follow those donkeys. He said pointing his finger. Hurrying she thanked him.

'Here take this'. She said giving him a bracelet from her hand.

'Don't beg anymore'. Saying she scooted. He bit it. GOLD!.

With the blanket over her head, Helena waded among men, women and children who were taking their supplies on their donkey's and cattle. Arriving at the port she saw there was a lot of commotion as crewmen loaded goods into ships to sell at other ports, women haggling with traders for giving fewer shillings, some fighting over spilling of cotton and maize on the wet ground. Helena bustled around beseeching about Captain Edmont. She was jostled but none paid any heed. Finally, the ship sailed away and one by one everyone left as commotion receded. The day was over, while even some talked about getting less shilling from the traders for their goods. It was already late noon still Helena wandered around the town asking everyone the whereabouts of Captain Edmont.

'That golliwog scoundrel owes me money'. One said.

'He died'. Said another.

'Sure got eaten by sea vermins'.

'Could be brawling boozed probably over a turtle at the dock'. A local folk said. 'Where?' she asked.

Helena reached an isolated place, a ragged tavern not far from the dock where all crewmen, Captain's and traders get boozed after sailing. She went in and smelled of salt and beer. Some stared at her, some whistled but none cared. Five men were gambling for a turtle on the table while most were sloshed as usual. She asked the bartender for Captain Edmont when all of sudden five men on the table started a fight. In no time everyone joined in as bottles flew high and splashed down, tables were overturned, and a few lay dazed on the floor.

'Sure you low with some pennies, Captain'. Said a beetle-browed man.

'Only when my pocket's full'. Said a chisel cheeked man storming out of the tavern.

The bartender pointed at him. 'that's Captain Edmont'.

Helena followed him to the dock where the Captain met two men anchoring a boat.

'Still not in high tide, Captain?'. Said a podgy looking bald man.

'He means you're sober'. A pale-looking man said

'Only if that scallywag in Eldrich had paid me more shilling's. Said Captain Edmont aggrieved.

'Nosy little prick he is. Lost a turtle ain't you, Captain?'. Said the bald man.

'Captain'. A voice called from behind.

He turned to see a woman whose face was covered over in a blanket.

'Ship ain't sailing lady'. He said pointing his finger up. 'full moon'.

Helena said she needed a ship and a crew and would pay for it. The three men ignored.

Taking off her blanket she asserted. 'I am Princess Helena of Nimbad and I'm willing to pay 100 gold coins for all'. The two men working on the painter line of the boat stopped and goggled. Captain Edmont not at all surprised said about strange things happening at

the castle.

'Your King doesn't know anything about the sea's and I ain't taking orders from anyone who never stepped out of their comfy'. He jeered.

'How dare you make such slander about the King '. She raised her voice, stiffening her shoulders then relaxed a bit. 'okay! 150 gold coins'.

The Captain still uninterested told. 'look I just sailed 200 nautical miles I don't need-'.

'200 gold coins'. Helena slammed.

The podgy looking bald man called and muttered something to the Captain. Then Captain Edmont asked her what she wants.

'Your ship and your crew sail to Malkith'. Helena told.

All three men stood stock still. The bald man muttered again to the Captain.

'Okay'. Captain Edmont said. 'Malkith or not we keep the gold. Once on board, you're no Princess. 'Deal'.

Deal.

Both agreed all three set sail for three days before arriving at port Eldrich. Captain Edmont and his two men went out to bargain some crewmen while Helena sauntered the marketplace. She stopped at one shop selling items that were once lost in the sea. The seller was an old crippled man who instantly recognised Helena and said he once used to work with the King and know's what now happened in the castle. Without saying anything he handed her a spyglass.

'It sees what we can't'. He whispered. Captain Edmont returned with twelve men.

The bald man grumbled. 'Gotta given that plonker more'.

'Yeah, but we got what we came for'. Said the pale looking -man nodding.

They were talking about a trader who paid Captain Edmont less shillings three days ago.

'You zapped a trader for five shillings over a beer'. Helena asked Captain Edmont.

'No, because I lost a turtle that day'.

Again all aboard with Captain, his new twelve men and Helena all set sailed north. The sky looked dark and threatening as all crewmen were drunk and tattered. Captain Edmont impassively steered the ship watching the waters closely. Helena felt like a plebian now. She no longer looked like a Princess, her yellow dress all worn out with ragged patches. Staring at the night sky, she thought about her father in the castle locked inside a dungeon and her mother somewhere among the stars just when the bald man came to the deck next to her drunk. He blabbered about Captain Edmont's past about looting other ships and even once sailed with her father to find Malkith but couldn't discover it. Helena immediately stomped her way towards the Captain.

'Think we made a deal'. She said furiously.

'Deal still stands for me'. He said steering the ship.

She started wrangling with the Captain of being a pirate and that Malkith never had existed. Suddenly a strong gush of wind stuck them with lightning and the ship was accidentally steered off course. A clap of loud thunder echoed as waters came splashing down the hull over the deck.

Captain yelled at his crew. 'wakeup you lousy ragtails. Cut the ropes, hoist the foremast up'.

The bald man screamed with the wind. 'haul the ropes. Cradle at the double'.

Captain Edmont yawed the ship to right, as the rain came hitting hard on his face. What seemed hours after much sway waters went still, the rain stopped and the sky turned from grey to black again. Helena's head spun around and stopped. She woke dizzied with the sun on the horizon, it was dawn. All crew lay on the floor haggard and wet. She saw her spyglass lying at one side. She held it looking at all sides. First, there was some moist air, squinting her eyes she saw a single stone tower looming ahead miles away. Calling she woke everyone up. First came the Captain and looked through. Tower of Malkith. But with his eyes, he saw nothing. Then it sank in him that the tower perhaps had some spell. Captain stood back and ordered his crew not to move further fearing the tower might be cursed. But Helena persisted that the only thing that can save her father is in that tower then without thinking jumped into the sea swimming towards the tower. Captain Edmont ordered his men to bring down the coracle. 'what we all waiting for, mates. we've got to save a Princess'.

Once they were on the boats, the Captain reached and pulled Helena up. The tower was amidst the sea like a small island, as they came close the spell got lifted and the whole tower materialized which almost touched the sky. Reaching the island, the bald man called to one of his crew. 'Azlan, anchor the boats'.

Another one just like his fellow pale-looking man stepped next to him.

He said. 'I'm not Azlan'. His appearance slowly transformed into wizard Izus. He had been all along with them as one of the crew right from port Eldrich. All stared at the green-robed wizard. He explained it was an imposter at the castle with the guards under his spell now and had followed Helena from the castle to port Eldrich before joining as one of their crewmen. Izus forcibly struck his staff down as the whole island shook beneath, and the tower slowly started to give away imploding at the top as rubbles of stone came crashing down. Atop a fire skinned dragon came out coughing a ball of fire struggling to get free. All stood below, their eyes peering at the mighty dragon being chained somewhere inside the tower.

'Strewth! That's a real dragon'. Uttered the bald man with eyes-widened.

The wizard told if all want to get out of this island, first they must kill the dragon and bring its heart which will bring his powers back. Because as a wizard he can't touch the beast. Captain Edmont ordered his men to return to the ship, bring all bottles and drums that still has booze in them and all the ropes they could find. The crewmen returned in boats saddled with drums of beer and long twisted ropes. They started to tie the bottles along the length of the ropes in a line. Once done all stood apart below the tower holding the ropes. The dragon crawled down the tower rattling the chain around its neck shredding more pieces of stone into the sea. It tore open its chain, finally freed landed down hard. The crewmen flung away the ropes over the dragon as it flared a fire but caught itself as drums placed under exploded leaving the dragon wincing in pain before falling down. Captain Edmont unsheathing his dagger strode towards the fallen beast, ripped open its heart and headed back to give it to the wizard. At the same time, Elena leapt to her side to unsheath a dagger from the bald man and made a run towards the Captain, snatched the heart from him and pierced it. Izus roared but the tower above which was already giving away came crumbling and a part of it fell on him. Captain, Helena and the thirteen men hurried back to the coracle rowing back to ship as the tower came tumbling down. The whole island with the wizard and the dragon sank down into the sea and was never heard of them again. Aboard Captain once again steered the ship to Nimbad. At the castle everyone's spell was lifted, the King was freed and the imposter was gone forever. Helena finally betrothed her prince. The King summoned Captain Edmont and his crewmen rewarding them. Helena kept mum about Captain Edmont's deeds as a pirate and so was the slaying of the dragon and the wizard which no one knew other than the King, Helena, our vainglorious captain Edmont and his thirteen men.

Months later captain Edmont and his thirteen men set sail crossing two seas. Ruskin, the bald man said. 'It's been 565 nautical miles Captain. Where are we set'.

Captain Edmont thrust him a map he brought from a shop in Eldrich and pointed the lost city of Malkith. 'hoist the foremast up. We set sail to the east'. He commanded.

'Aye!aye!Captain'.

And the ship coursed beyond the seven seas where it had never sailed before.

3

TALE FROM THE HILLS TO DOOMED KINGDOM (PART I)

The Kingdom of Baxtonbur enjoys the tag of hoisting the most celebrated festivities than any other Kingdom. The castle is often decked up to its finest that can skip a breath for anyone who just passes by. Miles away to the north, a path winds up to a small hill and to the forests beyond. This route is the only other way to enter the Kingdom safely if anyone feels they are being threatened by the enemy. Upon this hill is a home for a few who live with farm animals, cultivating fruits and vegetables which they sell to the local markets. Pretzel, a young girl looked down the landscape that had a clear view of the castle and local villages below. She would often imagine herself wearing a pretty dress, her hands over the shoulder of a handsome Prince, dancing around in the halls of the castle. But her mother gave strict orders not to prance around long in the market and get back home before twilight.

'Pretzel'. Her mother called. She ran back to her house which was

just at the tip of the hill.

'Looks there's going to be another party, mother. That's twice in a week'. Pretzel said.

'Yes'. Her mother said. 'and you are not invited'.

They sat at the table for breakfast. Some boiled cabbages, corn and salted yam. She asked many times why she can't go there, dress like everyone else. It's not like she is going to be a Princess. But her mother only frowned. Pretzel knew she'll be disappointed, so she never asks anymore. Whatever she loved her mother. Two days later the bustling of activity began. Many guards and Kings with their big horses marched down the road towards the castle. It is usual for everyone here to show outsiders their way to Baxtonbur. Pretzel sat in her house watching a long line of men in horses going below. Who knew how many times she talked to a King, or maybe a prince, she thought. It was hard to tell in which horse the King rides.

'Pretzel'. It was her mother. 'I'll be out till noon. Think we've to ask again Mrs. Platty for more bulbs'. She leaves the house telling Pretzel to watch the fields. An hour later Pretzel goes to the forest to collect some mushrooms and her favourite magnolia flowers. She heard some approaching noise when five men in their horses suddenly stop in front of her. One of them took his helmet off.

'young lady is this the way to Baxtonbur'. His voice was hoarse. Pretzel stood still, don't know what to say. Another one took off his helmet. He looked young and fair.

'Looks you scared off the lady. I told you we can take the longer

route, now we're lost. And you call yourself commander of the first merit'.

'what's my job got to do with this'. The commander replied sternly.

Shaking his head the young man looked at Pretzel who stood silent. He had dark brown hair, Pretzel noticed. He must be the prince. Well he is. He asked her again the route to Baxtonbur.

'go straight. Pass the fields that has three houses. Then turn left beside the house where five rows of haystacks are piled, again go left around a farm fence, then right on the first road going down side of a shack'. She paused as her voice cracked. 'there's a house at the tip of the hill, just take the road around the field'.

The two men look at each other and at all sides.

'okay'. The young man said. 'perhaps, it'll be an honour if you come with us to show our way down'.

Pretzel disapproves, but the look in their eyes felt like it was a command.

'don't worry young lady, our men will safely return where you please'. He said assuringly.

Indecisively Pretzel mounted up behind with the commander, as they went riding with the path winding below. They reached the gates of the castle but only the young Prince entered in, commander Skiles stayed behind.

'you're not going in'. Pretzel asked.

'I mostly watch the gates'. He said broadening his shoulders to

show his temerity.

Pretzel saw people come in carriages with magnificent horses, all dressed in their best. She could only gape. The commander noticed.

'I know of a dressmaker who lives not far here'. He said raising his brows.

Both now entered a small two-storey house and knocked.

Mr Kenley opened the door. 'commander Skiles. Come in. How may I be of your service'.

Skiles said he needed a dress for her niece, pointing at Pretzel. 'even a spare one will do'.

But Mr Kenley told them everything was sold. Just when Mrs Kenley came. She told me she has one dress of her daughter but she is sick now to go for the party. Mrs Kenley led Pretzel in to dress her up. Wearing a peach coloured dress, Pretzel came out.

'I knew the size would be perfect. Doesn't she look pretty, Mattis'? Mrs Kenley said.

Commander Skiles and Pretzel arrive back at the castle but Pretzel hesitated. Commander Skiles assured her to stay calm. 'you'll pass as much as a Princess does'.

Holding arms they both entered the great hall. She could see every Princess dancing with their Prince while all King and Queen talked and drank. Leading pretzel commander Skiles left her alone to find a Prince while he stood aside. Pretzel paced slowly, her body already twitching inside. Her mother would kill her for sure, she thought. At top of the stairs, she saw the brown-

haired Prince she came along with talking to the King .

'Your father was a great swordmaker. Best I've known'. The Kingsaid.

'He died two days ago'. Harlow said as he observed King's face contorting.

'My condolences, Harlow. I bet you're as good as him'. Saying the King excused himself.

Harlow for a second caught a young beautiful girl, their eyes met. Pretzel started to jog among the dancing pairs heading back to the door just when Harlow obstructed her.

'You seem kind of lost. You look familiar. Have we met before'. He asked.

Pretzel holding her breath saw the King coming down the stairs. Then suddenly the door burst open behind her.

'Mother'. She exclaimed.

Her mother followed pretzel as she got anxious after seeing her riding with some men down the hill. Then she looked at the King. 'hello! My brother Claytius'.

Pretzel stared at her mother as everyone stopped dancing, their eyes fixed at the two. King Claytius pretended not to know this woman, calling his guards to take charge. Commander Skiles drew his sword and pointed at the King when his men made a lunge drawing their own swords towards the approaching guards to shield commander Skiles.

King Claytius cried. 'what's all this about. This is madness'.

Pretzel and her mother watched in silence as everyone started mumbling.

Harlow spoke. 'this King of yours is a traitor. The woman here is your rightful Queen '.

He said about his father who on his last breath told how Claytius made him forge a dagger to kill the King . Claytius then killed Marlyn's husband before ousting her sister out of the Kingdom by accusing her of the murder of both her husband and father. Claytius's son Maniel unsheathing his poniard dived for Harlow, seizing the moment King's guards attacked commander Skiles's men. Many guards fell, while others fled. Harlow now had his poniard pointed at Maniel. As everyone around muttered and yelled. 'traitor'.

King cried. 'Marlyn, my sister stop this'. Skiles still had his sword pointed at him.

She said he was never her brother. She reminded him how her father found him orphaned but then decided to raise him as his own.

'He loved you more than me and you murdered him'. She said enraged.

King Claytius confessed how he realized that he could not be a rightful King and the throne will pass down to her sister Marlyn. That's why he killed her husband. There was more murmur now. Everyone wanted King Claytius hanged but Maryln put Claytius and his son Maniel in exile and told him never to set foot in Baxtonbur ever again. Claytius with Maniel left the Kingdom with the voice 'Traitor! Traitor! echoing from behind. Claytius turned back to look at Maryln.

'I'll have my avenge'. He said with bloodshot eyes. After that, no one ever heard of them again for a very long time.

Marlyn started to head back to the hills after instructing commander Skiles to lock away all treasures and sell away all items from the castle. Every King agreed to go in peace with Baxtonbur. Commander Skiles said some of his men from his Kingdom Klung will be called to protect Baxtonbur. Pretzel then married Harlow even if she knew that he was not a prince. Both stood gazing from the hills as the once-renowned castle slowly started to fade away.

4

TALE FROM THE HILLS TO DOOMED KINGDOM (PART II)

'Hold your left foot firmly. Now steady. Swing straight, point and attack'. Adrin did what he was told and finally had his sword pointing at his father's neck.

'That's my boy'. Said Harlow. 'just remember. Never-'.

'never let your opponent know about your strength. Yes, I know father'. Said Adrin nodding his head probably having heard it more than a hundred times.

'time for lunch'. Called Pretzel who was watching them for a while. 'and keep the swords outside before you come in'. Saying she went back in.

'There goes your mother, again'. Said Harlow putting the swords inside a barrel full of water.

'Can't you two give a rest? War is not due soon'. Said Pretzel arranging the table just as her mother Marlyn sat alongside who *looked pale but healthy.*

'You are right somewhat! But you'll never know'. Replied Harlow sternly before taking his chair.

'Not radish and mushrooms again, mother'. Said Adrin keeping a sombre face.

'You get to eat what we have, Adrin'. Said pretzel unrelentingly.

Harlow said glancing at him. 'don't ever argue with your mother, boy'.

Loud footsteps of a horse galloping echoed outside.

'I'll go have a look'. Marlyn said pushing herself up away from the table. 'probably it's him'.

She saw a long grey-haired man dismounting, with his sword dangling the side of the horse.

'Just arrived in time for lunch, commander Skiles'. Welcomed Maryln. 'come in'.

'Could've arrived soon'. He said. 'the pathway is not same it was before. The trees in the forest there now are all twisted and clogged up'.

'It's been a while since we heard a horse gallop'. Maryln said. 'Not many come and pass from here now'.

'Time has indeed changed'. Sighed commander Skiles.

'Now come in. Enjoy lunch with us'. Marlyn let him in first.

Commander Skiles first greeted Harlow and then pretzel before looking at Adrin.

'Oh! boy. I've been just a few weeks away. Now look at him'. Exclaimed Skiles. 'All grown up to height of his father'.

'Uncle Skiles. Did you bring that silver shield I asked last time'. Asked Adrin enthusiastically. Remembering the last time Skiles promised him to show his silver shield that saved him in the battle he once fought in lowlands at Klung.

'It's inside the saddle of my hors-'. Before he could finish saying Adrin ran violently outside oblivious to her mother calling after him to finish his meals first.

Pretzel put some roasted mushrooms, radish and corn on a plate for the commander and a bowl of turnip soup before settling next to her mother. Skiles sat next to Harlow.

'So any news worth hearing'. Asked Harlow sipping a soup from his bowl.

Marlyn felt a twitch inside her body. She knew which topic there were going to talk about.

'Nothing yet'. He said. 'but there might-. I say just there might be a word going around to invade Baxtonbur'.

'I knew it was coming'. Harlow said affirmatively. 'everyone knew that. Atleast had a sense of it'.

'I thought everybody went in peace with Baxtonbur'. Pretzel said suddenly confused.

'The mind of a man changes over time, Pretzel'. Skiles told. 'and it's been nineteen years since that day-'.

'That's enough talk for now'. Interrupted Marlyn with her eyes *looking down.*

'It's okay mother. Time has moved on now'. Pretzel calmed her mother.

Then Adrin came in, wearing a silver shield that hung loosely around his body. Sensing the mood around the table he sat down quietly. He knew what happened nineteen years ago, how King Claytius was exiled with his son Maniel after finding out about his alleged conspiracy over the killing of his own father and her sister Marlyn's husband for the throne of Baxtonbur. But Claytius accused his sister Marlyn of the murder ousting her out of the Kingdom. Pretzel told him every story about the hills and the Kingdom.

'Any news about him'. Asked Maryln quietly.

Commander Skiles knew about whom she was asking . 'Claytius and Maniel both have never been seen since then'.

'What is it there here now to invade. Everything here is ruined'. Pretzel questioned with doubt.

'Not everything. It's trade they're after. Everyone has an eye for Baxtonbur for its rich resources and landscape. Cotton, livestock, bread, corn, hills and rivers. Let's say Baxtonbur is centre for all trade'.

'Then war is imminent. Isn't it uncle Skiles'. Adrin said excitedly. All he did ever trained was in the fields outside the house with his father and sometimes with commander Skiles whenever he came to visit. He was desperate to go in for a real battle.

'You're not going anywhere, Adrin'. Pretzel assured him.

'Why can't ?. I can swing the sword faster than anyone. Father knows it'. Adrin said looking towards his father who stared back. He knew what he was going to say then looked at his mother glaring back at him.

'But uncle Skiles said there were boys younger than me who fought in battles before. And I heard all the castles have secret tunnels running all over the town'.

'Don't get too excited, boy'. Said Skiles. 'your mother is right. Besides, it could just be rumours floating around. In that case, there might never be a war'. Saying he stood to leave. Marlyn came behind him to see him off.

'I hope you're right. It better be just a rumour'. Said Marlyn. 'but just in case-'.

'My army are vigilant at all times'. He said foreseeing her thoughts. Then he suddenly stopped beside his horse, turned back as if he'd forgot something behind.

'I know you don't want to hear what I'm about to say, Marlyn. Still no matter how many men protect this Kingdom threat will always loom at large. The Kingdom needs a King and a Queen '. He mounted his horse and waved at everyone.

'uncle Skiles. You forget your silver shield'. Called Adrin.

'you can keep it, boy. It might be in use to you some day'. He then rode back into the forests.

Far away beyond nine ridges in a village, Maniel sat by the bedside looking at his dying father. Claytius lay with his eyes sulken and his body weared away beyond age.

'Maniel'. He hissed. 'remember our pride should not fade away in void. You must avenge for what we been through'. Saying he closed his eyes.

Maniel holding his father's hand tight said. 'I will, father'. His moist eyes and trembling face emoted anger for revenge.

The whole village was gathered to watch Claytius being taken away for burial. Three men made a bed out of dried leaves, straws and twigs for Claytius then lifted him to take to the burial site, as Maniel stood aside staring intently. Then he made up his mind.

Maniel arrived at a Kingdom made of unpenetrable stone. A guard stopped him and first went to inform KingSirius about the new intruder.

'I've no time to meet any low orders at this hour. Send away whoever it is'. KingSirius said steely to the guard.

'The man says he is the son of Claytius, sire'. The guard stated.

The King was rooted to the spot for a moment then nodded at his guard. The guard went out to summon the new intruder in.

A mid-aged man with unruly hair entered and didn't even bow before the King as a courtesy. KingSirius sat at his dias, shocked and speechless.

'Maniel son of Claytius. What a miracle it is to see you'. Uttered the King . 'pardon my words but you look all slipshod. How is your father'.

'He died two days ago'. Said Maniel glumly.

KingSirius mumbled something don't know what to say. Then he finally said.

'I haven't heard a terrible tiding in a long time. You must be feeling devastated. Tell me how I may be of service to you'.

'Your father and I had a strong mutual respect for each other. My condolences to you'. Said King Rowan. Maniel now stood at the great hall of the Kingdom Izog.

'Condolences are departed words right now, King Rowan. Now it's time to go beyond what's never been aimed for a long time'. Said Maniel diligently.

'What do you propose, Maniel'. Asked King Rowan curiously.

'Go to war against Baxtonbur. This is madness. All Kingdom will be against us.

You've been exiled Maniel. You must be living in a fool's paradise'. Said King Edil of

Osburg. 'besides what's left in Baxtonbur now'.

'Trade worth many years if conquered. Dams, rivers, iron, battle horses whatever you ask'. Said Maniel. 'Everybody knows Baxtonbur is the centre of all trade. Whoever claims it can have access to unlimited wealth for years to come'.

'We've been at peace for a long time, Maniel. We don't need any turmoil at this period'. Said King Edil.

'You can't be at peace King Sirius if there is a threat at large'. Answered Maniel.

'What do you mean'. Asked King Sirius suddenly becoming alert.

'I hear other Kingdoms are touted to go to war with Baxtonbur and wish to gain the wealth of trade all for themselves'. Said Maniel.

'Those are just rumours I've been hearing for quite some time'. Said King Rowan.

'what if it becomes true, King Rowan'. Maniel said sharply.

'I know for what you're here, Maniel. You want revenge for your father's death'. Said King Edil.

'I want to see the Kingdom torn to pieces. I don't want to hear the name Baxtonbur anymore'. Cried Maniel.

'We do not need a war. Anyway why do we want to see our Kingdom crumble against thousands of armies that'll be against us'. Said King Edil.

'You don't have to fight other Kingdom's army Kingsirius'. Said Maniel. 'what all King of other Kingdom's have to do is become allies and charge towards the gates of Baxtonbur'.

'In that case, they'll have no choice. The only Kingdom now left to protect Baxtonbur is Klung'. Said King Sirius impatiently.

'Even if we overthrow the Kingdom what becomes of the trade you speak of. Who'll claim it'. Said King Rowan.

'Everyone my lord. Each King gets equal profits from the trade'. Said Maniel. 'all we've to do is invade Baxtonbur and share its wealth among the Kingdom's before one of them claims to take it all away and the glory'.

'What you get with all these Maniel'. Asked King Sirius.

'I want the Kingdom to fall and be doomed'. Maniel said. 'besides all can still have peace as you always had'.

King Sirius thought for a moment and arranged to summon all other King of other Kingdom's for a council.

'Double the guards, General Kaul. Plant all your men you got. We need to protect the Kingdom at any cost'. Said commander Skiles to General Kaul of Baxtonbur.

All the men from Kingdom Klung and armies of Baxtonbur lined themselves up taking charge to eliminate any threat from outside. Men started surrounding the ruined castle of Baxtonbur, local markets, the hills and the forest.

'Return to your homes. It's not safe outside'. Ordered men riding in their horses to the folks wandering on the streets.

Commander Skiles dismounted and entered Pretzel's house.

'Commander Skiles, what's all these happening'. Pretzel came rushing quickly.

But Skiles said nothing. Everyone knew what he was going to tell. The most terrible outcome they all dreaded for a long time. Commander Skiles took himself a chair to sit.

'So, it has all begun. Isn't it'. Said Harlow as if anticipating this moment.

Regaining her posture Pretzel asked again. 'tell us everything'.

'A week ago there was a council at eleven rocks'. He said softly without hurrying. 'King's of all Kingdom were there and they all agreed to join as an ally to invade Baxtonbur'.

Pretzel listening intently almost shrieked.

'And it is true what they are after'. He continued. 'And all have decided to share their profits of trade among them'.

'Who were all present at the council'. Asked Harlow.

'Everyone. That's what my men told me. Kingsirius, King Edil and King Rowan'.

Harlow could only stare. Adrin's impulse to fight literally died down hearing what Skiles just told now but he still had the urge to fight in a battle.

'There's more news'. Said Skiles reluctantly. 'Claytius is dead'.

Maryln suddenly lost her breath grasping for air before regaining herself.

'How'. She managed to ask with her voice shaking and feeling a lump in her throat.

'I don't know how but it was nine days ago, my men brought me the news'. He said. 'and Maniel was present at the council too'.

'Maniel'. Repeated Harlow. 'What was he doing at the council'?

'Guess it's his doing after what has now just started'. Skiles told.

'Obvious and expected'. Maryln said finally.

Before Pretzel could say anything Skiles sensed what she was about to ask. He said.

'It's anticipated that Maniel may have wanted to take revenge for what we did to him and his father nineteen years ago. We put both to exile so he now wants to see us fall'.

There was a long silence now between them.

'I'll try to bring more news'. Skiles said. 'Of course, depending on the circumstances about to occur'.

Then he left. That night none spoke much at the dinner just prayed for a ray of hope to shine on Baxtonbur.

Harlow tightened the silver shield around Adrin's torso. 'there you go, my boy. Now that'll hold long enough for you'.

Pretzel just watched as her mother sat at a corner praying. Commander Skiles was out waiting with his horse ready. Finally came Harlow and Adrin to admire their new horses which Skiles has brought along. Maryln stayed at the door while Pretzel came running towards her son Adrin.

'You can come home anytime Adrin. Just be-'. She struggled to speak.

'Don't worry, Pretzel. He is braver now than I had ever known before'. Harlow completed what she was about to say then he kissed her on her forehead, waved to everyone and disappeared into the path leading towards the forest. Pretzel's eyes turned watery waving back after they were long gone. 'Just come home soon'.

Men erected tents to make camps on the periphery of the forest then started to make fires as stars twinkled at the night sky. The smell of stew, potatoes, corn and brewing tea engulfed the air. A few men had brought a bottle of rum to warm themselves on this cold night. A guard waded his way out of the forest to glimpse a barren field stretching miles away ahead of him. Standing at the edge of the forest he could see small dots of light glowing on the other side of the field. It is here where the battle will be fought. The tall guard returned to his camp to confront commander Skiles what he had seen.

'They have already set their camps. And we're a little laid back'. Skiles felt conscious of how fast the enemy moved closer to them.

'which means only one thing. The battle will be fought early maybe even tomorrow'. Said Harlow a little bit surprised.

Commander Skiles and General Kaul knew they must make preparations soon.

The next day when the sun was at its highest, commander Skiles, General Kaul and Harlow waited at the edge of the forest with only ten men behind guarding them with their swords ready. If Skiles was right men on the other side too must have known about their camps set last night. They waited patiently for close to an hour. Far afield fifty men with armours, swords and spears arrived coming in with formation and stopped. Behind them came the three Kings: King Edil, King Rowan and King Sirius riding with their horses along with Maniel. A guard went to King Rowan who handed him a scroll then he started coming towards commander Skiles's side. Seeing the guard arriving, Skiles men positioned themselves in front of him. Commander Skiles waited and signalled one of his men to move forward. Both the guards met as the other guard handed over the scroll. The man came back and gave the scroll to Skiles. He opened the scroll and read the message. "To commander Skiles and his company. If you still want to avert the war this is your only chance. Accept your defeat and we promise the casualty will be none. Otherwise, our brute force of army already outnumbered against yours will show no mercy".

Commander Skiles announced the message to all his men. He said.

'if anyone wishes to go home this is your call. No offence brave men but your will whatever it is will be your decision'.

'we already made our call commander when we arrived here. There ain't turning back now'. One of the guards said.

Commander Skiles wrote his message on the scroll and handed it to his guard. He went again to hand over the scroll to the other guard who was waiting for the reply.

King Rowan read the message. "The last chance it will be then. Will fight till last". King Rowan passed the scroll to King Edil and King Sirius as Maniel's face turned red. The three King and their company started to retreat back to their camp disappointed. Maniel turning back his horse gave a sharp look towards commander Skiles and Harlow before moving along with them. Both sides now departed to their respective camps. That whole night Skiles and his company didn't sleep and kept working their plans on how to face their enemy with an army that was clearly double their own.

Adrin waited alongside with bated breath glancing both sideways. Commander Skiles was to his right who kept his umoved eyes ahead intensely. His father Harlow was to his left, he looked and just nodded. Adrin understood what he was going to say. All his memories flashed before him. The gardens, fields and farm animals back at his home. His mother, Pretzel waiting patiently for him smiling. He turned back to see if his grandmother Marlyn was watching them closely from the hills. But all he could see were pine trees hovering and swishing behind him against the wind. The sweltering heat from the sun above was keeping them warm. Adrin saw everyone's sweat dripping down their neck who had stationed themselves with hundreds of horses equipped with bows and arrows, their body and face covered in iron with armours, helmets and wielding long spears. All stayed motionless. Adrin tried to remember his training with his father and commander Skiles in the fields at the hill. But the heat made him impossible to think. Far away at the other side of the battlefield thousands and thousands of men stood with their armours shining silver in the sun. Adrin let out a small gasp. A loud blare of honking was heard. King Sirius raised his hand making a move as only six hundred of his men charged forward. King Adil and King Rowan did the same as six hundred men from each stormed ahead together riding in their horses. Commander Skiles raising his sword too rode along with General Kaul taking with them only five hundred of his men. Adrin gripped tightly the rope around his horse to go but was stopped by his father.

'patience, my boy. You will have your turn'. Harlow said stopping him with his hand touching over his silver shield.

Adrin felt the ground beneath shudder as if it was going to give away anytime. Hundreds of men with horses came close to face each other with wind pressing against them. The three Kings sat in their horses watching the moving fleet. Maniel stood beside giving a little grimace. Perhaps this was the end of Baxtonbur, he thought. The sound that came was that of iron being smashed into the mountain. Even the horses that were stationed back whined as the sound echoed. Harlow and Adrin watched the scene as Skiles's men drove through the enemies formation. Spears pierced into the flesh of horses which winced in pain as men were thrown out into the air. Skiles rode furiously carrying the sword which tore the flesh out of the bodies of their enemy Then there were the arrows that kept flying everywhere striking everyone into their chest and neck. A guard of King Edil went for Skiles's horse, cutting down its legs. Skiles flew high then fell hard on the ground as the sword went free from his hand. The guard clutching a sword came close towards Skiles. He bent down to go for the kill but Skiles grabbed an arrow lying by his side and forced it into the guard's throat who collapsed over him. A horse with his hind legs kicked a man as he went flying before falling down smashing his face and breaking his shoulders. One of Skiles men had killed more than seventeen men and was still wielding two swords in his hands dripping with blood. He went for the two men who were going to attack General Kaul. He threw his sword which went through one of them right into his chest. General Kaul alerted killed the other man. He turned towards the man who saved him.

'Nooo. . . behind you'. General Kaul screamed. But it was too late.

A man came riding from behind waved his sword in an arc which made the guard's helmet fly high into the air. The guard kept gazing at General Kaul as blood leaked from the back of his neck. Then he fell down. The man mounted on the horse stared at General Kaul instead of going for a kill he retreated to join his fellow guards. Raging with anger General Kaul ran and doubled over to see the guard had stopped breathing. His open eyes stared at the sky. General Kaul saw all his men falling helplessly. The King's men started rounding up who were without weapons before killing them all at once. General Kaul knew it was time. Grasping for his breath commander Skiles surveyed the battlefield as the enemy came in close. He glanced towards Kaul. General Kaul stood with difficulty, raised his sword high and screamed. 'make way for the lions'.

Harlow heard the call. On the other side, Maniel felt satisfied. For a moment all three Kings sensed victory. Then soon all the anticipation of victory over Baxtonbur disappeared.

The men surrounding the Skiles men suddenly stopped and looked skywards. Arrows came swooping like rain hitting over them right through their armours. There was a tense feeling of confusion among the Kings. Maniel too felt the same. Just as more than hundreds of men emerged from all sides of the forest shooting arrows. Harlow shouted to his remaining men stationed to advance. Adrin's pulse raced full as he rode with all his might. The King's guards stood motionless, not knowing what to make of this. Now it is they who were being surrounded by Skiles men inside as well as men from outside. The enemy finally started to step back a little seeing the men they were about to kill were now making their move. But the Skiles men have ambushed to make it impossible for them to escape. The horses came hard right over the enemy crushing them to the ground making them squeal. The men who had no weapons to wield took the arrows lying around striking the enemies forcefully. Still, the King's men fought with all energy finding gaps and wounding with their spears which penetrated into the flesh. Some of King's men started fleeing into the forests but were shot down with arrows. Still, some managed to escape. Maniel already furious called to the Kings.

'send all your army. What are you waiting for'.

But none of the Kings made any move. All the stationed men stood puzzled looking at each other wondering why their King didn't make any call. Seeing no reaction from them Maniel shouted towards the stationed guards

'Move on you fools. Your brothers are dying out there'.

Sensing no reaction from the guards he rode alone towards the battlefield. Only fifty men followed Maniel while others waited for their Kings command.

The King's men were already retreating but were unable to do as Skiles's men completely surrounded them. Adrin swayed his sword hitting some of King's guards bruising and thrashing them all. But none he seemed sure he actually killed. Commander Skiles came riding on a horse; stopping before Kaul and Harlow who both worked as a team to keep the enemy out.

'Make sure none leave the battlefield. Keep tight our flanks as they are. That way we'll keep pressure on the enemy'. Saying he drew his sword thrashing one coming at him. Then he rode towards the men who were now arriving with Maniel. Harlow and Kaul kept their momentum clearing out anyone who came near them. That way their men will have more advantages to kill the enemy easily. Maniel galloped with his horse killing King Edil's own few guards on the path. He swirled his sword to break the formation held by Skiles men. King Edil, King Rowan and King Sirius watched in pity as their men were being driven out. This is not what they wanted ever. The battlefield started turning into a bloody massacre. Adrin seeing Maniel thrashing his men ran towards him before picking a spear lying by side of *him and threw into the air. The spear missed Maniel by inches from the side of his abdomen. Maniel's eyes remained fixed at Adrin. He dismounted from his horse, gripping his sword tight charged towards him. Their swords clashed making a clinging noise. Adrin keeping his body firm swung right and left moving along with his feet ahead. But Maniel was strong enough to dodge all the moves as his sword made a cut into Adrin's right shoulder. He winced but kept fighting, he dived and ducked, at last, made a slash on Maniel's arm. Maniel stepped back to check the bleeding. Again he pounced as both fought ruthlessly. Commander Skiles kept thwacking with all energy as Harlow who lost his sword assaulted men using his bare hands. General Kaul now deeply wounded still welted a blow killing one of King Sirius's guards. The sword in Adrin's hand flew out of his hand. Maniel seeing an opportunity here tried to strike the sword right into his chest. Just in time Adrin moved backwards but fell. The silver shield saved him bruising a little. Adrin without a weapon managed to get up lamely and saw Maniel approach brandishing his sword. Maniel suddenly stopped and whimpered, glancing down to see a sword had struck him. Commander Skiles stood behind. Maniel lunged but was again struck by Skiles, whining he fell dead. Several of King's army finally gave up. Commander Skiles gazed towards King Rowan. The King raising his hand high dropped the sword then turned his palm downwards. It was a sign to accept defeat. King Sirius and King Edil did the same before heading back to their camps. One by one all of the Kings army left the battlefield. The battle was won. And Baxtonbur was saved. Skiles men howled having had their victory. General Kaul was wounded and died in the battle. The sun was almost down but both the armies again came to the battlefield to carry the body of the injured back to their camps. Both the sides didn't utter a word just carried their tasks. One of Skiles men struggled to lift a injured fellow bleeding from his back. King Edil's guard came and helped him than just giving a nod headed back to his company. It took two days for Harlow, Adrin and Skiles to arrive back to the hills. Pretzel and Maryln waited outside the house for them to arrive. The emotion was suppressed but Pretzel just sat down and cried. Days later at eleven rocks all three Kings, Harlow and commander Skiles were present to sign a treaty of peace. But one minor problem existed that to sign the treaty a Kingdom must at least have a King or a Queen to a throne and Baxtonbur had neither. Later the treaty was signed. But now a grand ceremony was organized at Baxtonbur after a long time. Preparation to restore the castle began. Every King , Queen and elite were called upon to welcome a new King and Queen ascend the throne. Harlow sat at the throne with his King's crown. Pretzel became the Queen and Adrin the Prince of Baxtonbur. Maryln sat at the dais beside them delighted to see both take the throne. It was the wish that was inside her for so long to see Pretzel what she always wanted as hundreds of people cheered. She was now the rightful heir to the Kingdom. But for Pretzel her home was always where she belonged back at the hills and knew even without the throne Harlow, Marlyn and Adrin all could still have lived back there happily forever and ever.*

5

A SONG OF ETERNAL RING

'I found it'. Said Tori.

'No, I found it first'. Said Lori.

Two little fairies were arguing for a ring they found in the woods.

The third one, Feri said. 'oh! let's not fight for what isn't ours. We take the ring to Orin. He'll decide'.

Orin, a dwarf was the chief of the woods where all magical creatures lived. Orin was in a council with his fellows in a giant oak tree when the three fairies entered. Orin greeted all three:'tori the blue, fair but ignorant; Lori the green, wise but insouciant and last Feri the white, young but frivolous'.

Lori said. 'Orin o'wise I found this ring but this ignorant one you say it's her'.

'It is. I found it in the first-morning sun'. Said tori raising her voice.

'You lie'. Lori barked.

'Doesn't change when you say that'. Tori intoned.

'Oh! stop'. Orin cried. 'there's always some trouble when it's you three. Popin lost an eye because of you all'. Popin, a one-eyed troll stared.

Orin examined the green rock.

'Fighting for a thing that barely fit in your fingers'. He said to all three fairies.

It must be from the castle, he thought. He sent Cori and Pepi, two pixies to survey the woods.

Popin said. 'Orin o'wise you speak like something is going to come after us'.

'I hope not'. Orin replied grimly.

'Orin O'wise you're not going to punish us, are you? asked Lori softly.

'That my little dinkies, depends on circumstances about to happen'.

All three fairies stared at each other.

In the castle of Evador, Queen Esmeralda was furious about what happened last night. Wearing a green fur robe she paced back and forth.

'Find him'. She ordered General Horg. 'And the ring'.

The Queen was now in her room lost in thought when her daughter Aurelia entered. Even if she stood facing her back

Aurelia could see her mother looked sullen.

'Stop grieving mother. It was never your fault '. She sympathized.

'Now's not the time, Aurelia. I'm not in a state to hear any composing words. It's not like I have a chip on my shoulders. But I swear by the Mighty Moon of the Last when I find him my blade will pierce his heart'.

Trolls, wood sprites, brownies and dwarves all gathered at the oak tree looking at Orin. Much has happened by now. Three dark-robed hooded men came riding in their horses, seized the ring from Orin and also took along with them two pixies: Cori and Pepi, who went to survey the woods.

'Poor creatures. Said a snub-nosed troll.

'No doubt men from Boldur '. Said a cross-eyed dwarf.

'What do we do now'? Asked Popin anxiously.

'I want to know what has befallen us, send Dorin to the castle'. Said Orin imperatively.

Queen Esmeralda still in her green robe stared blankly out of the window. A pang of new guilt took over, strangling her slowly like a chain being tightened around her neck suspended by a big rock. A week earlier, the Queen was riding alone to the east side of the castle into the forest when she suddenly fell down the steep earth after her horse tripped with low thickets. A Rider from the north was just passing by.

'You can ride with me or I wait with hope till your horse returns'. Said the Rider.

Evador had no King. King Leon died of an illness when Aurelia was a child. But the Queen still had the blushes of a young Princess and instantly fell for the charm of the stranger. For seven days the rider stayed in the castle entertaining everyone with his adventures. Last night the rider said he has some errands and must meet his fellows.

'I promise. I'll come back'. He said.

But the Queen insisted he stay one more night. Around midnight, the rider stood by her bed watching her sleep. He cautiously took the ring from her finger kissed her hand and sneaked out of the room unseen out of the castle to Boldur. At dawn, the rider was nowhere and the eternal ring was gone.

At mid-noon, Horg's men came with a lanky jolly-go young man dressed in green attire. A long white feather was pinned to his green hat, a quiver and a bow hung over his shoulder. He struggled between the two guards.

'Let go, you warthog. One arrow is all I need to poke your eye out.

'One more word greenie, you go to croc-infested pit'. Said a grim-looking guard.

'What's all this General Horg? The Queen arrived with Aurelia by her side.

'My Queen, our men found a wanderer riding in the woods. He claims he saw three dark-robed men riding north'. Said General Horg.

Queen Esmeralda eyed the lanky man long before she spoke.

'Last night something was stolen from the castle. Something-'.

She paused then said. 'precious. Tell me what you saw in the woods'.

The young man was about to speak when the Queen interrupted him again.

'Oh! my manners, please. Tell me your name. What's your errand here'.

The man said. 'I'm Jorvett Umpton. You're right my Queen, I'm not from here. I come from the south. An archer am i. I go places seeking adventures'. His voice now was more sonorous. 'i travelled far through mountains and dark tunnels. Battled foes and monsters and even killed a half-breed with a single arrow. Finally on my last day rested in Elwigs village. By the way, folks there eat mountain oysters'.

'Tell me about the three men'. Queen exclaimed.

'Oh! yes'. He told how he was riding with the wind when he saw three dark-robed men.

'Men riding from another side'. He said imitating the scene. 'i almost knocked out their horses'. He waved his hands mimicking horses. 'By Jove! Big horses I've ever seen'.

General Horg asked. 'Men you saw, were they in black'.

'Tall hooded figures. Empty face'. Jorvett said.

General Horg knew it. 'men from Boldur'.

The Queen said. 'Your horse will be taken care of, wanderer. You must be famished'.

'By Jove! Yes'. Jorvett replied excitedly.

'To dungeon'. The Queen just gave a look at Horg before leaving.

'No, wait'. Jorvett protested but the guards obeyed General Horg and locked him inside a dungeon.

'Now get used to some dark, greenie'. Said the grim-looking guard.

Dorin, a flying creature perched atop the high window of the castle saw it all then flew out to the woods.

Far away in north atop a grey tower a dark figure rose from the dais and gazed towards east beyond the horizon. Waiting to regain his glory. 'Now, where is my rider'?

It was late-night, Aurelia sneaked to the dungeon where a guard slept at the entrance of the archway. There was no gate. Taking a torch on side of the wall Aurelia passed slowly down the stairs below. She moved between empty quods casting her shadow all over. Thinking some kind of monster had entered Jorvett cried.

'Come no near you ghoulish creature. I've slain many like you'.

'Where are you'. Aurelia whispered.

'You dare look right. uhuhh. . . '.

She turned right as the torch shone at his green eyes. He could see the golden curls of hair on her shoulders. Celestial.

'Princess'. He muttered.

'See I'm no monster'. She said.

Jorvett stood upright wreathed in smiles. 'i was just being alert'. He said pompously. Aurelia told him about the eternal ring the rider stole from the Queen . A ring that bids fate to whoever claims it: good or evil.

So the Queen thinks I'm some sly from Boldur '. Jorvett said.

'My mother isn't taking any chances'. Aurelia replied.

Queen Esmeralda feels a chill and wakes up dizzied to see smoke engulfing all around her. She stands upright and starts to walk to realize it's a stair, moving straight up before disappearing in thick fog. Ahead a grey tower loomed above her. The tower of Boldur . She peered in front of a large iron gate half-opened. She entered and found herself inside a long empty hall. As smoke begin to recede she saw large statues of sentries at either side of the stonewalls recess. Far at the other side, a door opened and a dark hooded figure emerged. Standing barefoot her body went cold. Lord Death himself appeared.

'At last, we meet'. His voice gave a hiss.

He approached with long bony hands dangling from his robe. His face gave a skeletal look. He gave the Queen a choice: you can have the ring only if you become Queen to Boldur or give me all the wood creatures else I'll bring death to all. 'Make a wise choice'.

Again smoke engulfed her. The Queen woke up breathing hard. She went to look out the window to see the moon was full. Only it was not a dream. She realized how much Evador has changed. Once all realms were ruled by wizards, sorcerers, warlocks and magicians until men took over. A great wise wizard foresaw and realized the age of wizards was over. So the wizard made Leon, a great wise King to rule Evador giving him all riches and the eternal ring for everlasting peace. Some sorcerers went against him and one cruel sorcerer killed the wise wizard. A terrible battle began until only the last one was left, the cruel sorcerer then ruled Boldur . Some creatures betrayed him and dwelt in the woods since then. Now the sorcerer awaits to regain his lost glory. His realm.

The rider presented Lord Death with the eternal ring. 'You're late'. Said lord death.

Rider explained how he left the castle that night but had to stay in the woods only when his men arrived at dawn. He also said about the wanderer and how they lost the ring before retrieving it back from the woods.

'You've done well Aronan, the rider. You'll be rewarded. Now you and the Queen can rule Boldur '. Said the lord.

'But my Lord it's your realm'. The rider said.

'I'll be invincible. Now that I have the ring. It'll bid my command'. He held the ring high which turned red. 'i've other world's to conquer now'.

Cori and Pepi were locked in a tiny cage somewhere inside the tower of Boldur.

'Look what you have done. I say we wait at the willowy tree but you went to explore that thorn hedge and now we'll be-'. Saying Cori cried.

Cori and Pepi went exploring the abandoned thorn hedge but were captured by rider Aronan and his men.

Suddenly Pepi squeezed out of the cage.

'Come back, you dumb gubble. It could be cursed outside'. Cori growled.

Immediately Pepi then grabbed and pulled Cori out of the tiny cage, and the next moment they were fluttering in the dark between columns and arch doors of the tower.

'Ouhhh! I'm going to faint in this darkness'. Cori whimpered.

They found a large half-opened door and heard some voices inside. They saw a tall well-built man standing ten yards away before a dark-robed figure sitting on a stone dais.

'Come let's look close'. Said Pepi.

'Is this not close enough'. Cori sneered.

They went in and lied doggo behind a gargoyle at the side of the door. Cori was gripping the hand of Pepi tightly.

'Stop it'. Pepi complained softly. 'you're giving too much light'.

'What. It's just my wings'. Cori said proudly.

They heard the sorcerer sitting on the dais saying how all other Kingdoms were going to join Boldur for the battle against Evador. Pepi and Cori came out and sat high inside the mouth of a gargoyle.

'I think Orin sent us out for a reason. He knew we'll be caught'. Pepi said.

'We got to tell Orin'. Cori said. And they flew out to the woods.

'I've never ventured out of Evador'. Aurelia said drawing her

knees up as she sat listening to Jorvett's adventures in the south.

'It's getting late. I must go'. She said promptly.

'Wait. Princess'. Jorvett called.

'The name is Aurelia'. She said.

'a-u-r-e-l-i-a'. He repeated. 'are you named after a-'.

But she left and promised she'll come back. Aurelia, he muttered again.

Coming out Aurelia took the key from the guard who was still sleeping. The next day before noon everyone was assembled in Queen's hall. Orin, the dwarf was called upon along with the three fairies: Feri, Lori, Tori and two pixies: Cori and Pepi. Orin told the Queen about Cori and Pepi's escape from Boldur who heard the plot about every Kingdom joining to wage war against Evador. Queen Esmeralda thought of her dream, she knew all wood creatures will become slaves to the sorcerer once she becomes the Queen of Boldur . She ordered general Horg to prepare for the battle and the battle began with all Kingdoms against Evador. Even little wood creatures fought bitting, jabbing and gnawing the enemies. But Boldur was easily outnumbered against Evador. Many men fell as enemies charged to the gates of Evador. Queen Esmeralda ordered General Horg to defend the gates till last before departing back to the castle. She opened a casket that had a sword inside made by the great wise wizard himself. With the sword held in her hand, she quickly rode to Boldur. Meanwhile, Aurelia was left alone in the castle and every guard was out defending the gates. She entered the dungeon, opened the quod and was out of the castle with Jorvett *as they went riding in their horses far east.*

'Where we going'. Jorvett asked.

'A place you're not going to like'. Said Aurelia.

Aurelia and Jorvett came to a barren land where nothing but only huge rocks more than a dozen protruded from the ground. All rocks had a narrow hole at its base. Suddenly a shadow covered them. To their dismay, they saw ten-foot-tall troglodyte peering at them. It made some stentorian sounds as one by one many troglodytes started to come out from holes of the rocks. Jorvett and Aurelia could only watch. Till now nobody knew they existed, betraying the cruel sorcerer as wood creatures did, the troglodytes hid in here unseen from others. Only Queen Esmeralda and Aurelia knew about them. Rumour was that all wizards and sorcerers gave all riches and gold to King Leon but he instead gave them to troglodytes who had no liking for such things. But no gold was ever found in Evador and now the sorcerer has conjured all Kingdom's for gold in Evador, so when Evador falls he will then conquer other Kingdoms too. Queen Esmeralda arrived at Boldur , entered the long hall where the sorcerer sat on his dais supported by his white staff. He looked at the Queen and then at the sword with astonishment.

He said. 'Sword of the wise wizard. Hmm. . you made a poor choice, you can still save those creatures'.

'And enslave them all. Never'. She said with blood rushing wildly in her veins.

'Don't you know that all these realms are all mine? Until a puny

living soul like you came and stole everything.' Lord death roared with fury in his eyes.

'You are no better than us. Like you we don't murder our own people, but you did'. Queen Esmeralda said stiffening her shoulders.

Lord death became enraged and began to force himself up but the Queen lunged forward first as her sword clashed with his white staff. Jorvett and Aurelia stormed out of the forest to Evador blazing away their arrows. Troglodytes came crashing through the trees thrashing the enemies and hurling stones at them. Finally clobbered the enemies started to retreat from the gates. The sword was no match as the sorcerer's staff broke into a two-piece. He knelt down with the Queen pointing the sword at his chest. He gave a mocking laugh.

'I'm no mortal. To kill me you must utter my name and no living soul has ever known a sorcerer's name'.

'But I do'. She said. 'LEMESVORTEN'. And pierced the sword into his heart.

His body shrunk and convulsed as black smoke rose before exploding into thin air. Aronan came clutching his sword, bloodied in battle. Queen Esmeralda stared at him a moment. He ran forward but fell face down. Behind General Horg had struck him with an arrow. Queen Esmeralda picked the ring from the floor which turned green again as dark clouds above receded for a new dawn to begin. Every Kingdom went in peace with Evador as their spell was lifted cast by the sorcerer. Back at the castle, the celebration has begun. Jorvett was made free to wander any realm he willed. The Queen then called the three fairies: Lori, Feri *and Tori before her.*

'The Queen knows our name'. Uttered the three fairies.

She placed a tiny diadem on their head for their courage in the battle. In the woods, the great oak had fallen during the battle. The Queen presented Orin with new seed for a home tree that grew so big that all creatures lived happily forever. Princess Aurelia married a handsome Prince from the west and sang songs of all things as she is called the singing Princess. But that's another story.

6

A SONG OF WHISTLING WOODS

In a far farmland village, Verona keeps her family afloat by selling flowers. Like any other day, Verona crossed the bridge across the river that divided the village and the dark forest to go to another town. One day as she was returning, she saw an old withered woman standing on the bridge helplessly. The old woman confronts she is blind as a bat and had lost her way to her house. Little did the poor girl know she had been lured by the ragged old woman. Approaching a dark twisted wooden house under an old tree, as the woman said Verona lead her inside. It was twilight, the old woman offered Verona a drink. As she drank it she fell on the floor dizzied. She woke up the next day in her farmland house puzzled. Verona resumed her chores helping her mother and putting flowers from the garden into her basket and leaves the house. Again on returning Verona sees the old woman, help to lead to her house has a drink and wakes up the next day in her house without any recollection of what happened before. The same happens on the third day. On the fourth day, Verona

refuses the drink. The old woman confesses that she was once a Queen and a witch has cursed her because she was cruel and arrogant to others as she was beautiful like no one. And now she was left to live in this miserable life. The woman said in the Kingdom, the King couldn't recognise her and she found solace alone in this forest since. She explained the curse can be broken by a potion made out of a young beautiful girl. On the first day when Verona visited she used her hair; on the second day a sleeve of her dress and on the third day she used her nails to make a potion but all failed. Verona noticed now her missing sleeve.

'I'm destined to die in this wretched house'. The old woman said with moist eyes.

A day later, Verona visits the old woman's house and gives her a flower of Aurelia. A rare flower said to cure any ailments, considered for good luck and everlasting happiness.

The old woman exclaimed. 'where did you get this flower'. Shocked to see a flower of Aurelia in hands of a flower girl. Verona told Princess Aurelia presented the flower to her grandmother as a gift for the help and care for her folks after the battle of Boldur.

'You can keep this flower'. Verona said.

The old woman was overwhelmed by this gesture as tears rolled down her eyes. Verona returned home elated. Verona gave the flower Aurelia to only those who are in great need and takes back on the third day as it is said the flower can cure any sickness in three days. Months passed, the once desolated Kingdom ruined in the war was again built to its former glory as the new Queen ascended to the throne. But the guilt of arrogance takes her all over again with her cruel tyranny of huge taxes and customs. The new Queen visited Verona in her farmland village as gratification.

She reveals. 'I'm Queen Claudia. And I forever will be grateful for your gratitude'.

Verona remembered the old woman she met, now she looked young and beautiful again. A week after, some soldiers march to Verona's house, arrogate all the flowers of Aurelia and leave a bag of gold upon Queen's command. Verona's father feeling morose buries the bag of gold in the backyard of their house. Now all flowers of Aurelia adored at the Queen's Kingdom. One day Verona entered the town to see all townfolks in utter chaos. Ruffians and local thugs plundered the Queen's castle. Verona asks one of the folks who said that the Queen was poisoned and was dead. Days pass, word got out about Verona's deed for the Queen. All Kings and folks people from every Kingdom gather for a council and crown Verona as the new Queen. A handsome Prince from the south came and married Verona in a grand ceremony.

A destitute man and a woman with their child beg for mercy to the new Queen for their wretched life. Queen Verona told them to go to a farmland village, her own house. The destitute man was working with a dibble in the backyard of their house when he finds a round bag. A woman arrived carrying her child.

'Look'. He said to his wife seeing a bag full of gold. 'we're saved. We never have to beg anymore. Long live the Queen !'. And they lived forever happily.

7

A SONG OF MYSTIC VALLEYS

Never there was a leap of joyous jamboree in the Kingdom before, as King Leon and Queen Esmeralda welcomed their first child. Many elites came from far away to bless the child, who was as white as the moon and blushed like a flower. One day a maid saw a butterfly looking insect with big wings pricking the hand of the child. The spot it bit turned purple. She came out rushing to the Queen and said her child has been bitten by thingamabob, as locals called it. As it generally doesn't bite children, an instant bite on grownups could be death. Queen Esmeralda sobbed in distress. Both King and Queen visited every village and town to help save their child. But all said the bite of a thingamabob cannot be cured. Holding her child Queen cried like never while the King sat hag-ridden. King Leon even announced rewards who can help cure their child. When all hope was lost, a local elderly woman visited the Queen. The woman said for their child to be cured, they must travel far to the valley of holies and bathe the child in waters as holy as they could find. She also told the child

has to be cured in seven days or will die.

'I'll go even if it's the end of the world'. Said the Queen.

Carrying their child, the King and the Queen travelled days between mountains and rivers, crossing ridges through the path of forests and lakes until they arrived under the valley of mystic looking hills. The waters flowed majestically in every crevice. They begin to ascend the hills that had rare herbs and flowers they had ever seen. They could see waters clear as crystal snaking all over the valleys. Tired they took rest among exotic flowers and plants as water showered from above. The Queen remembered the woman warning them not to take anything from the valley or drink other than their child. Queen Esmeralda walked among the flowers as white like her, knelt down with her child and bent one of the white flowers as the waters in it dropped and touched the lips of her child. Both King and the Queen sat for a while when suddenly a white-maned four-legged creature with a long curved horn walked towards them. With its small blue face and blue fur body, it sniffed the child as if given a blessing, then it stepped back and with its mouth plucked a nearby white flower, dropped it and waging its long white bushy tail disappeared into bushes. Queen Esmeralda picked up the flower, she noticed the purple spot on her child had vanished and was white now. Her child has been cured. King Leon and Queen Esmeralda leapt in joy with no bounds. They bathed the child with the holiest water in the valley. Queen Esmeralda didn't know it was a dream or what they had seen. Something told her to name her child Aurelia. The name of the white flower. Years later a whole lot of Aurelia flowers adored the castle of Evador. It was said when Princess Aurelia sang, all those are sick felt rejuvenated. Now taking the flower with them King Leon and Queen Esmeralda returned to their Kingdom elated.

8

ELLA FOREVER

Ella and Nina had become best of friends almost inseparable. While Ella was a Princess to the Wulfang Kingdom Nina was just a girl who did small chores at the castle. Coincidently both were six years old being born on the same day. Nina's father was a fine craftsman and was very close to the King . When Nina lost her mother early King Lubius took pity and raised her in his own castle. Ella and Nina grew up together playing and exploring the castle. Sometimes they would just wander around local markets but mostly went to the lake to catch fish. Ella's father would often get annoyed with the two who always get into some kind of trouble. When they were nine both trying to explore out of the Kingdom got lost in a forest only to be found again when the King with his guards went looking for them. In spite of a warning, they spent so much out that Ella's father had to send his guards to bring them back. The only time Ella and Nina are not together is during bedtime. Nina and her father both lived just outside the castle where small houses were built for potters,

craftsmen and blacksmiths.

'Mother, why can't Nina sleep with us in the castle'. Ella asked lying in her bed.

'Because Nina has to sleep with her father'. Replied her mother drawing a sheet over her.

Stars twinkled in the sky as the full moon appeared out of grey clouds.

'Mother, the moon looks so lonely. I want to keep it always by my side'. Ella said.

'Someday you will. Now go to sleep'. Said her mother kissing her forehead.

For some reason, Ella was very obsessed with the moon wanting it forever spellbound by its white light illuminating the whole night and the stars around. Like moon was some kind of treasure waiting only for her to open it.

'goodnight, Nina. She said looking out the window then went to sleep.

Many summers and winters passed. When the snow arrived it would make impossible for the traders to come to the Kingdom or a strong gush of wind and rain would splatter hard down threatening to fill up farms, lakes and tunnels. A hundred and twenty-year-old giant tree fell down at the castle planted by King's Lubius great-great-grandfather that stood like a good-luck charm for many generations. But now some twenty to thirty men were lugging to take the tree outside the castle to the forest.

'father, not again'. Ella said stamping her feet hard. 'I've told this many times before'.

'Ahhh! please Ella. For once act like a Princess'. Her father said looking tired. 'Eva, you talk to her'.

'Your father is right, Ella. At least try to show some courtesy before the Prince when he arrives'. Her mother said.

'But I'm only seventeen mother. I'm not ready to get married'. Ella said frustrated.

'Nina dear, perhaps you can talk her out'. Eva said calling to her. Nina stood watching them silently then suddenly become alert.

'Guess your father's right, Ella'. She hesitated to find for words. 'i mean someday you'll be a Queen '.

Ella was a little surprised to hear Nina referring to her as the Queen. She never before called her in any courtesy way but her name.

'Besides, it is just an engagement'. Nina continued. 'Not like what you think you'll be actually marrying the prince, are you'. Saying she let out a laugh.

King Lubius and Eva both turned and stared at her. She went quiet.

Summer arrived and the castle was all lit up and decorated to its finest. Guests started filling up the castle, the lawns, and the gardens. Many varieties of meals, desserts and drinks were being set up outside as servants and maids attended to relish people who came from far away.

'So what you think the Prince will be like'. Nina asked wearing a green dress sitting beside Ella as two maids dressed her hair.

'Sure dumb-witted disarrayed and scathed'. Ella in her yellow gown said rolling her eyes. The maids adjusted her few hairs to make a braid.

'i heard they are supposed to be charming, intelligent and handsome'. Nina said doubtfully.

'only in fairytales'. Both said at the same time.

The Prince had arrived and was talking to the guests at the terrace of the castle. While at the lawn below meals were being served with some music and band being played along. A few even started to dance as others joined in. Ella and Nina were prancing all over the lawn trying new desserts and drinks before joining with others to the music.

King Lubius watching them muttered to himself. 'that girl will never grow up'. As Eva studied the King's face.

The Prince saw two girls frolicking and hopping along with guests, but his eyes were glued to a girl dressed up in a green shimmering gown.

'Who is that'. He asked curiously to his personal attendent Mr.Mattis.

'That lady is the King's only daughter'. Mattis said. 'the one you're going to marry'.

The Prince kept staring amazed by her beauty and charm.

Finally the Prince met Ella. Nina walked alongside after being insisted by Ella to be with her. All three strolled silently for a while in the garden.

'You two seem kind of close to each other'. The Prince spoke first.

'Well we are'. Nina said. 'we grew up together and are best of the friends'.

'Pardon me please'. The Prince suddenly became ashamed. 'I should've introduced myself first. I'm Prince Rupert of dunes'.

'I'm Ella. And this is Nina'. This time Ella spoke.

'It's wonderful meeting you both'. He said delighted bowing a little. 'Ella and Nina'. Then kissed both their hands.

Mr Mattis voice echoed from behind. 'My lord. Excuse me for interrupting. But you have been called sir'.

The Prince looked at the two ladies feeling disappointed and ashamed again.

Before he could say, Ella and Nina bowed excusing themselves first making way for the Prince to attend his meeting.

'Oh! Pardon me ladies. Let me introduce myself to you first. I'm Prince Rupert of dunes'. Back in Ella's room Nina swayed both her hands imitating the Prince and started giggling.

'stop it, Nina'. Ella said. 'He was nice and behaved well like one should before a lady'.

'And you were blushing'. Nina whispered.

Ella opened her mouth to speak but came nothing. 'No, I wasn't. She said abashedly.

'yes, Ella. And you're blushing now too'. Nina said softly becoming interested. 'So tell me what you liked about Prince Rupert. I noticed his green eyes'.

'He had brown hair. Long and soft'. Ella said little excited.

'And'. Nina persisted.

'He had a clean and fair cheek'. Ella continued.

'And'.

'He looked sturdy and the dress he wore matched his green eyes'.

'And'.

'And'. She stepped back a little as if trying to run. 'Think I may have to put a ring on his finger'. Nina shrieking dived towards

Ella hugging her hard excitedly.

The ceremony for the engagement began at the long hall of the castle as hundreds of guests waited eagerly for the Prince and Princess to arrive. Prince Rupert wearing an embellished red tunic and a red trouser came first and waited before at the marble dais as several guests whistled and cheered. Everybody went silent when Ella came with Nina walking to her side on a woollen red carpet laid out separating the guests. . A little girl came forward and gave Ella a bouquet of daffodils. Ella then began to place her feet up the dais when Prince Rupert stopped her.

'Wait. You are the Princess'. Rupert said bewildered.

'Yes'. Ella said a bit surprised.

'Princess Ella, the only daughter of King Lubius'. He asked again.

There was already a tense moment among the invited who started murmuring to each other. Even King Lubius and Eva both seated became unsettled looking sideways.

'Who is she then'. Rupert asked pointing towards Nina who stood nervously after being pointed out in front of everyone.

'She is the daughter of my father's loyal craftsman'. Ella answered quickly.

The Prince stood shaking his head, his feet moving back and forth.

'I thought she was the Princess'. He declared furiously. 'if she isn't then the ceremony is not happening'.

Ella astonished stood where she was. Nina was shocked and confused.

King Lubius tried to persuade the Prince to sort out the misunderstanding that was caused. Everyone now began moving towards the dais to confront the cause of this situation. Eva lost her breath and collapsed on the floor before Nina helped her back to the seat. Looking around and suddenly becoming anxious Nina shouted. 'Ella. Ellaaa. Elllllaaaa.' There was more confusion now as King Lubius desperately called his guards. The flowers of daffodils lay sprawled to the floor. But Ella was nowhere and was gone.

Ella furiously ran towards the forest stomping her feet wildly into the mud. How far she came after running away out of the castle she didn't care. It seemed like hours but still kept her pace oblivious to what lied ahead that might make her trip and fall off in the dark. Coming out into clearing a mile afar she saw a mountain with a citadel like structure atop. Climbing hard up the road she arrived at the top to see a century-old dilapidated castle surrounded by a three-foot thick wall. The moon was glowing brightly than ever. With the cold gripping tight she went inside the ruined hall of the castle which seemed like its been burned down. Cobwebs and broken statues lay everywhere as the ceiling printed with murals were faded to dirt. A chandelier lied at one side completely shattered. Ella saw a light flickering below a closed-door at end of the hall. The door opened without giving any creak. She entered slowly inside to see there was a fireplace *burning in the corner. Dark and warm feeling tense she took small steps surveying the empty room that had only a wooden chair close by the fireplace.*

'This place is ain't for any heart-ling strong or weak'. A voice echoed.

Ella startled spun round to see an old withered woman standing at the door. Half-crouched she wobbled a little supported by a wooden staff.

'If you still want to live like a free bird go back the way you came'. The woman said in her croaked voice. But Ella remained unmoved intrigued by the old woman thinking what might have held her here all alone.

'Who are you. I can offer help if you need'. Ella said sympathising with her.

'I don't need any touchi-feelin' all that rubbish here'. She screamed. 'if you want your heart to be where it is, leave now'.

'I've come far away and I'm not going anywhere'. Ella tempted stood where she was. 'unless you tell what you doing here'.

Sensing no fear from the girl the old woman came near to see her face close. She had blue eyes and a round face with puffed pink lips. The eyebrows were in a perfect arc like it was made by a brushstroke. The flickering fire that shone on her golden hair made her look even beautiful. The old woman studied her knowing who she might be. But didn't say any.

'You seem lost. I see no fear inside you'. The woman said walking to the fireplace. 'But beyond those eyes is an emptiness raged and deprived. Seems someone has not loved you as you wanted'.

Ella stood stock still. She tried to remember how after seeing the Prince felt for the first time in her life that someone not close to her is going to love her forever. But soon all hope vanished within a shell.

'You are a witch, aren't you'. Ella said with her widened eyes. The woman didn't reply.

'Can you teach me a spell'. Ella exulted ran towards her. The old woman seeing her approach yelled. NO. DON'T YOU DARE COME NEAR ME.

The woman started to storm out of the room but Ella kept drawing near persisting her to teach to some spells. CAN YOU RIDE A BROOM.

The winding stairs spiralled high above as both arrived at the top of the citadel. The roof in this empty room was missing as the moonlight shone through the hole. Ella gazed at the moon as her chest pounded amazed by it is the size which now looked even bigger. The old woman could almost hear her heartbeat, all the way thinkingshe had a pure heart. A witch can kill anyone but not those who have a pure heart. But hearing Ella's heart racing faster she realized there was something more inside her she don't know yet.

Many months passed, somehow Ella persuaded the old witch to teach her the spells. She now knew the wooden staff the witch carried was not any staff but a magical one that clogged all the spells she tried on her. Ella kept breaking things and smashing the walls but still did her best. She even dusted some books and scrolls doodled with writing and pictures showing how to perform spells. One heavy discoloured book had a picture of the moon shining over a figure standing with hands wide open.

'What's the moon got to do with a spell'. Ella confronted this to the witch.

The woman sitting beside the fireplace felt shocked.

'How in the leshy's horn name did you know about that'. She asked. Seeing Ella remain silent it was obvious she had learned it from the books she gave her.

'I'm not going to teach you that. That's the most powerful spell ever'. She said sternly. 'You can even turn blind trying it'.

'The book says unless a witch who knows is killed by another'. Ella said giving a malicious look.

'I should never have let you teach my spells'. The woman said forcing herself up from the wooden chair. But Ella's fuming eyes were already glowing with menace.

A bright green light came out from Ella's hand hitting the witch who defended with her wooden staff which vibrated. Ella using her other hand summoned a spell as flames at the fireplace began to behave violently. The sparkling fire tried to shroud the witch drawing her inside. The witch fighting hard not to lose uttered a spell but it was too late as flames of the fire had engulfed her completely and dragged her into the fireplace. Like a splash, a bright light exploded followed by a scream as the whole place shuddered then stopped. Then an invisible force flashed before Ella making her fall backwards. Slowly she got up and saw the witch was gone but some kind of force had entered her making her feel different inside.

Reaching the top of the citadel Ella saw the full moon illuminating white light. She realized that the moon was the source for the witch's spell who drew the power from its light making her strong and live for many years. But first, she must summon the spell that was lingering in her head for a while. Now recalling the spell from the books Ella stood raising her hands wide feeling the moonlight take her over. The light glittering over her made her look like an angel. Above the clouds moved threateningly and the sky grumbled somewhere as the darkness gripped all over making the stars and the moonshine forever. And for the first time sun will never rise again. Everywhere trees withered and birds swooped down falling from the sky. In the forest, a stag ran wildly and collapsed down. A pack of wolves whistled and moved madly before attacking themselves. Days passed, Ella became more and more strong who now stood gazing atop the citadel beyond the dark horizon. King Lubius, Nina with some guards wading their way out of the forest glimpsed the silhouette of a mountain a mile away. They arrived at the top of the mountain in cautious movement with the moon being the only light showing their path. They entered the hall of the citadel which gave a scary look as every corner was in pitch dark. Out of nowhere a big green smoke of light moving like a cloud appeared over the ceiling above them. They saw broken pieces of statues and rubbles of stones lying everywhere.

'This place is ain't for any heart-ling strong or weak'. A voice echoed.

All turned to look towards where the voice came.

'Ella'. Nina exclaimed. King Lubius was overjoyed watching her appear suddenly.

Nina began to step closer but stopped midway instantly.

'You should never have come here'. Ella said calmly.

'Ella, what has happened to you'. Whimpered Nina.

'Come home, dear'. King Lubius said with grief.

Nina observed she wore that same yellow dress from the ceremony.

'Ella, come back. There's nothing here for you'. Nina tried convincing.

'You're wrong, Nina. There is much more in here for me now than what I wished'. She said proudly.

Ella then glanced towards the guards who stood behind like sentries as if there are in danger of being attacked.

'You come here with your guards to take me away with force'. Angered Ella addressed her father.

'No, Ella. They are here for you. To take you back safely, dear'. He said concerned.

The guards seeing Ella raging with temper begin to move nervously clutching their swords tight. Ella sensing that the guards were going to attack her cast a spell striking them. All flew high in the air hitting against the wall then fell down. The spell was so strong the whole hall shook and the ceiling started to give away slowly with falling debris. King Lubius and Nina moved unsteadily before losing balance on their feet as the floor vibrated. Suddenly all the walls begin to collapse showering dust and rocks everywhere as the ceiling came crumbling down. Nina got up slowly from the floor and saw King Lubius lying unconscious. She tried to move between the debris and saw a winding staircase going up. Atop Ella stood looking fixedly as Nina emerged from behind.

'Ella, you have to stop this. Look what you done'. Nina said losing her strength.

Ella kept looking steadily beyond as the moon gleamed above her.

'See for yourself, Ella. We have not seen the sun for days. Everything is dying'. Nina said breathing hard. 'think about your mother, your father. No one can live like this'.

Ella turned slowly meeting her gaze with Nina. She slowly stepped forward and touched Nina's face with her hand as a drop of tear dripped on her fingers. Then she went back to stand where she was.

'Isn't that look beautiful'. She said looking up at the moon. 'i always dreamed about being close to it'. She begins to step back a little more.

'Ella, no'. Nina cried. 'Don't do this'.

'Now it no longer will be. For I wish to be close so I can almost touch it'. She stepped back even further. Nina cried, ELLA. NO. PLEASE.

She stood almost at the edge and beyond the cliff there was nothing.

'Goodbye! Nina'. Then she fell dropping below into the deep darkness. A burst of yellow and green light exploded with sparkling dust as a white beam of light began to rise up moving towards the moon before disappearing into the darkness. Slowly the dark clouds began to clear as stars faded and the sun appeared blessing the darkness with a bright flash of light. In the castle, King Lubius and Eva grieved for their daughter for days and months. Nina back in her home stood gazing at the moon with tears rolling down her eyes. She imagined Ella was somewhere on the far side of the moon. Many months passed, a bright beam of light appeared from the sky striking deep into the forest. A figure rose dressed all in white glittering like a crystal as her white hair sparkled like stars. She was the Princess of the moon who now headed towards the castle back to her Kingdom. Ella had come back.